W9-DEF-770

RADSPORTS GUIDES

SNOW SKIING

TRACY NELSON MAURER

Rourke Publishing LLC
Vero Beach, Florida 32964

www.rourkepublishing.com

PROJECT ASSISTANCE:
Jon Strasburg moved to Jackson, Wyoming, after graduating from the University of Wisconsin-Eau Claire. He swabbed the resort toilets at night to pay for his lift tickets during the day. A proven new-school downhill skier and snowboarder, Jon also honed his aggressive mountain-bike riding skills and performed in commercials.

In addition, Joel Rosen at 1080skiboarding.com and Source Skiboarding Apparel in Boston, Mass.; Heidi Jo Viaene, Ski School Director at Spirit Mountain, Duluth, MN; and the staff of Ski Hut in Duluth, MN generously shared their expertise.

The author also extends appreciation to Mike Maurer, Kendall and Lois M. Nelson, and Harlan Maurer.

PHOTO CREDITS:
Pages 4, 11, 17©Nathan Billow/Allsport; pages 18, 31, 35, 37, 38, 43©Mike Powell/Allsport; page 21© Didier Givos/Allsport; page 24©D. Troutfire; page 27©Eyewire; page 33© Jamie Squire/Allsport; page 42©Al Bello/Allsport

EDITORIAL SERVICES:
Pamela Schroeder

Notice: This book contains information that is true, complete, and accurate to the best of our knowledge. However, the author and Rourke Publishing LLC offer all recommendations and suggestions without any guarantees and disclaim all liability incurred in connection with the use of this information.

Safety first! Activities appearing or described in this publication may be dangerous. Always wear safety gear. Even with complete safety gear, risk of injury still exists.

Library of Congress Cataloging-in-Publication Data

Maurer, Tracy Nelson
  Snow Skiing / Tracy Nelson Maurer.
    p. cm. — (Radsports guides)
  Includes bibliographical references and index.
  Summary: Surveys the history, equipment, techniques, and safety factors of snow skiing.
  ISBN 1-58952-105-6
    1. Skis and skiing—Juvenile literature. [1. skis and skiing.] I. Title.

GV854.315 .M38 2001
796.93—dc21   2001041645

Printed in the USA

TABLE OF CONTENTS

Get past the beginner stage and the mountains are yours.

WIMPS DON'T SKI

Skiers take risks. This leaves most wimps behind in the ski lodge. Those few wimpy souls who follow their friends onto the slopes usually quit after a few crashes or when their toes feel chilly. Fast or slow, real skiers know this sport takes guts, skill, and smart choices about the risks.

Real skiers also know skiing is fun and exciting!

chapter
ONE

CURES FOR THE CLUELESS

Knowledge cures the clueless. Learn about the equipment and types of skiing you can try.

Cross-Country Skiers

Cross-country, or Nordic, skiers use poles and long, skinny skis to glide across the snow. The boots clip into bindings only at the toes, leaving the heel free. You can walk or run almost normally in these boots. A fairly easy sport, Nordic skiing is a good way to exercise outdoors. Very good skiers may become racers or **telemark** skiers. Telemarkers rip down steep alpine slopes. Some even hit jumps for tricks.

Downhill Skiers

Downhill, or Alpine, skiers use poles and skis with curved-up tips to quickly carve "S" turns down the slopes. Trick skiers, or jibbers, sometimes use twin-tipped boards that curve up at both ends. This allows them to hit jumps backward or forward.

Stiff boots hold the feet and ankles in place. You walk like a duck in these boots. Bindings anchor the boot toes and heels to the skis. But they release in a hard crash to avoid serious injuries.

Body form, control, and speed define your skill level. Advanced skiers might try huge ski jumps or racing. Other hard-cores include freeskiers, who charge down rocky chutes or hunt big air, and hotdoggers, who pulse through bumps called **moguls** or launch tricks off jumps.

Skiboarders

Skiboarders ride short, wide, twin-tipped skis. The skis look like snowboards that shrunk. The non-releasable bindings work with regular hard-shell ski boots. Real skiboarders do not use poles.

Some people say skiboarding feels like in-line skating on snow. It's easy to learn. Your grandma can probably get air the first day. Most kids can take small jumps after a few hours.

SNOW SPORT	EQUIPMENT	TRICKS	RACING	WHERE
Cross-country, Nordic Skiing, or Telemarking	Long, skinny skis Long poles Very, very soft boots Toe-only, non-releasable bindings	Rarely	Yes	Groomed trails Backcountry
Old School Freestyle Skiing or Hotdogging	Long, skinny skis Poles Hard boots Releasable bindings	Yes (No grabs)	Yes	Moguls Man-made jumps In-area backcountry
New School Freeskiing	Short, wide skis Poles Hard boots Non-releasable bindings	Who-yah! (With grabs)	Depends on course	Half-pipe Man-made jumps Snowboard parks In-area backcountry
Skiboarding (so new it has to be New School); Wrongly called snowblading or snowskating—"Snowblades" are a brand of skiboard	Very short and fat twin-tipped skis No poles Non-releasable bindings, Hard boots	Yes (With grabs)	Not often	Half-pipe Man-made jumps Snowboard parks Rarely backcountry
Snowboarding	One very wide board, can be twin-tipped No poles Hard or soft boots, Non-releasable bindings	Yes (With grabs)	Yes	Half-pipe Man-made jumps Snowboard parks in-area backcountry

With your ski boots on, step into the bindings at the rental shop. Practice releasing the bindings. (What if you need to get out of them quickly to use the bathroom?)

TRY BEFORE YOU BUY

Anyone can ski. But don't sink money into ski equipment before you try the sport. Rent from the ski resort or sports shop.

Tell your outfitter that you need beginner's equipment. Your athletic ability and physical fitness will also help the outfitter decide on the length of skis for you to try. When you stand next to your skis, the tips should come up higher than your chest but lower than your forehead. This still gives you plenty of length to tame.

Your outfitter will find ski boots for you that fit tightly around your foot and ankle. The boots tilt forward a bit. You'll feel the boots pressing on your shins, not on your calves.

RAD TIP

Don't carry hot chocolate while wearing ski boots, especially climbing up or down stairs. Practice walking in your ski boots across solid floors until you can clump along at an even, steady pace.

TRUTH AVOIDS PAIN

The outfitter moves the bindings to fit your boot size and sets the binding tension to match your height, age, weight, and skiing ability. Tell the truth! The binding's tension setting guides the release function. In a crash, your bindings automatically pop up. You want your legs free to react to the impact. Boots locked into the bindings can force muscles and bones to twist in different directions than your other body parts. This makes skiing less than fun.

In the past, ski bindings used leashes like snowboards do today. Now bindings come with two small metal shafts, called brakes. Brakes poke down into the snow when the bindings release. Brakes prevent skis from zipping down the hill without you.

BUYERS, BEWARE!

When you're ready to invest in equipment, the pros say to buy boots during the season for the best selection of sizes. Look for end-of-season sales or pre-season "ski swaps" for savings on used and new skis. Check the used equipment very carefully, especially bindings. Ski shops can't work on dated bindings. Ask an expert if you're unsure.

The "savings" on used equipment could cost
you an arm and a leg if the bindings fail.

Skiers usually carry a ton of gear with them because the weather and snow conditions can change quickly. One huge bag may be filled with:

- Ski boots
- Goggles
- Helmet (many ski clubs require them)
- Wax
- Transceiver
- Shovel
- Ski gloves or mitts (more durable than normal winter gloves)
- Neck gaiter (not scarves: scarf tails choke you if they tangle with the chair lift, trees, and even passing skiers)
- Face masks
- Walkie-talkies
- Probes

Another long, huge bag may be filled with:
- One pair of poles
- One pair of skis

FUNCTION BEFORE FASHION

Some snobby skiers think that snowboarders dress for fashion (how something looks) instead of function (how it works). Today's younger downhill skiers wear the same gear that snowboarders do. The gear looks good and works hard. The materials are usually extra strong, water **resistant** and warm. They handle wipe outs all day long, day after day, without ripping or letting you walk around with a wet backside.

DIG THE KNUCKLE-DRAGGERS

Function plays a big part in the mitts or gloves. Snowboarders, skiboarders and jibbers who swipe their hands into the snow for balance while they turn and land jumps earned the nickname "knuckle-draggers". Join the knuckle-draggers club only if you're wearing heavy-duty snowboarding gloves or mitts. Otherwise, you'll shred your ordinary winter gloves by the end of the day.

RAD TIP

On very cold days, try instant heater pads inside your mitts. These small pads look like tea bags. A chemical reaction inside the pad fires them up to a toasty 135°F (57.2°C) or more. It's like carrying a little furnace with you. Look for them in the ski shop or at sports stores.

CHILLING FACTS

Heat escapes your body four different ways. Stay warm by blocking the escape routes and layering your clothing.

Method of Heat Loss
1. Evaporation: Perspiration or sweat
2. Radiation: Heat passing to colder air
3. Conduction: Surface contact
4. Convection: Air movement, such as wind

Heat Keepers
1. Wicking fabrics next to skin
2. Hat, leggings, turtleneck, wool/fleece sweater
3. Thick gloves, snow pants, warm pants
4. Wind-resistant outer layer

LAYER YOURSELF

What's the smart way to stay warm? Dress in layers. You sweat even in bitterly cold air, because you burn energy controlling your skis and moving your body. Start with clothing that wicks moisture away from the skin. Wear fleece in the next layer. Then put on waterproof, but breathable, jacket and pants.

Avoid denim and other cotton next to your skin! In very cold weather, cotton can kill. It traps sweat. The sweat freezes and forms an icy layer that drains down your core body temperature. The body starts to shiver.

Shivering comes from really tiny, fast muscle movements trying to make heat. Shivering means you need to go inside. Drink something warm to help raise your core temperature toward 98.6° F (37°C). Climbing uphill on skis or exercising also makes heat if you're not near the ski lodge. Don't wait. **Hypothermia** sets in quickly. Victims become cranky, sleepy or dazed. They may pass out. Hypothermia can even kill.

MORE DANGER LURKS IN THE COLD

"Frostnip" attacks your ears, nose, cheeks, hands, and feet. Painful, white patches blossom on the parts farthest from the body's core.

"Frostbite" does more serious damage than frostnip. Frostbite freezes the skin tissue and destroys muscles. Skin with frostnip or frostbite needs a slow warm-up, or you'll make it worse.

DUMBER TO DUMBEST

You already know smoking is not a good thing to do. Smoking when you're cold is even worse. It causes blood vessels to tighten and slow your blood flow. This makes it harder to stay warm.

Drinking alcohol is also a dangerous thing to do. Drunk skiers can't react fast enough to changing risks—like nasty trees that jump out at them.

TAMING THE BEASTS

You have the guts. You have the equipment. You're dressed cool (warm). You bought a lift ticket. Now comes the fun part— gaining skills.

Don't cut corners here. Start with lessons. A qualified instructor, such as an instructor certified by the Professional Ski Instructors of America, helps you build your skills quickly and safely. Your instructor will show you how to control your speed and direction. You also learn tips to avoid the major flubbers.

chapter

TWO

Every **newbie**, or new skier, begins on the gentle bunny hill. This small slope is the best place to tame those beasts beneath your feet.

Most instructors suggest that you avoid the poles for awhile. Poles just add more equipment to untangle when you crash.

SOME NEWBIE BASICS

1. Centered Stance

Center yourself with your knees bent, legs slightly apart (not too far) and body weight slightly forward. You also want to keep your head and shoulders facing downhill. Your lower body directs the turns, not your upper body.

2. Wedges

Bring your tips together and make a "V" so that the point pushes through the snow. Wedges can help turn and stop. Put extra **pressure** on your big toes to dig the ski edges into the snow. Pretend you're squishing a spider with your big toes! When you progress to the larger slopes, you connect your turns across the hill to make big "S" curves.

3. Ski Skating

Put the ski tails together and tips apart like the opposite "V" of a wedge. Push off to the right and glide. Then push off to the left and glide.

4. Tucking (Not)

Ski racers squat down low and crash the gates. Most ski hills will kick you out if you tuck and fly straight down the hill. No bombing!

Ski skating helps you cross flat terrain. One of the best ways to learn this technique is watching other skiers. Pro cross-country skiers do it better than most.

Ouch! Even professional skiers eat it sometimes. You know what they say, "If you're not falling, you're not pushing the limits." Don't be embarrassed.

5. Gravity Tango

Newbies tango with gravity over and over again. As a new skier, you will fall. Don't fight it. Know how to fall and get up again. You'll enjoy yourself more and prevent injuries.

When you fall, tuck your thumbs into your fists. "Skier's thumb" is a common injury. A skier often tries to break a fall with his or her hand, but the thumb pokes into the snow. Then body weight hammers it down. A ski pole can work like a lever to twist the thumb even further backward.

Twisted knees and banged up elbows also keep the ski patrol busy. Fall toward the slope of the hill rather than away from it. You stop faster and with less twisting motion.

To recover from a fall, sit on your bottom with one hip leaning hard into the slope. Put your feet together, with the skis pointing across the hill—not pointing down the hill. Use your arms to push yourself away from the snow and upward.

THE BALANCING ACT

Skiing takes constant balance. You adjust your balance with every turn, every move. From powder (or "pow"— fresh snow) to crud (guess), snow conditions can change your balance in a hurry.

FOUR DIRECTIONS CONTROL BALANCE

Forward or backward balance comes from your feet. Think about where you feel pressure on your feet.

Lateral or side-to-side balance comes from your feet and your lower body, especially in a turn. The speed and size of your turns can change your lateral balance. The science and techniques of carving turns can take years to master. Enjoy the challenge.

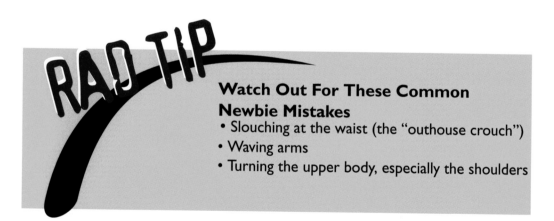

RAD TIP

Watch Out For These Common Newbie Mistakes
• Slouching at the waist (the "outhouse crouch")
• Waving arms
• Turning the upper body, especially the shoulders

Skiers try to carve smooth, even turns. Here, a skier makes "first tracks," the first run down a slope after a fresh snowfall.

EXERCISE REGULARLY

Skiing takes some muscle flexibility and strength. Exercise regularly and you will improve your skiing. Squats especially build strength in your thighs, or **quadriceps**, for greater control and better form.

STRETCH IT OUT

Before you hit the slopes, stretch your muscles. The pros do. With your ski boots on and your skis off, try these stretches.

1. **Squat Stretch**

Plant your feet about shoulder width apart. Keep your heels on the ground. Bend your knees and hips, pushing your seat out with your back flat. Exhale as you squat down. Inhale on the way up. Repeat at least ten times.

2. **Hamstring Stretch**

Don't forget the hamstrings, or the backs of your thighs. Bend one knee and extend the other foot forward as you exhale and lean forward. Keep your toes pulled up and heel down. Your head stays up. Feel the stretch and hold it. Then switch legs.

3. **Quadricep Stretch**

Plant a ski pole ahead and slightly to the right of your body. Hold it with your right hand. Use your left hand to grab the left boot heel. Pull the boot gently up to your seat. Tighten your stomach at the same time to keep your back straight. Feel the stretch and hold it. Then switch legs and hands. Finish with a few more squats.

REAL SKIERS SKI

Read about skiing. Watch ski movies. Most importantly, ski. Many of the skiers you see in competitions started skiing at age 3 or 4. They hit the slopes every chance they get. Some ski 200 days a year or more. Don't expect results overnight. Skiing takes time to master.

chapter
THREE

TUNE YOUR SKIS

Flip your skis over and check the bottoms. Look closely at the metal edges. The edge **bevel**, or angle, dulls after five full days of skiing. For about $12, you can pick up a small tool that files the burrs, or metal hangnails, off the edges between tunings.

If the bases look chalky white, they need a new layer of hot wax. The kind of wax changes for different kinds of snow. Waxing is both a science and an art. Don't mess with it until you're seriously into skiing.

Your local ski shop can tune the skis best. Your ski base and edges will cut into the snow better and carve tighter turns.

Tuning skis takes a professional touch. Sharp metal edges carve better turns. Smooth bases glide faster over snow.

SKI SMART

Remember that courtesy counts, especially on the ski slope. When you purchase a lift ticket or season pass, you agree to follow the resort's rules. You'll see the **Responsibility** Code posted at every ski facility in the U.S.A.

Ski smart and you lower the risk of hurting yourself, hurting others, or killing yourself. The total number of ski accidents have dropped in recent years. But serious injuries and deaths have climbed. Head injuries, most often from hitting trees, cause most of the deaths. Wear your helmet!

YOUR RESPONSIBILITY CODE

1. Always stay in control, and be able to stop or avoid other people and objects.
2. People ahead of you have the right of way. It is your responsibility to avoid them.
3. You must not stop where you obstruct a trail or are not visible from above.
4. Whenever starting downhill or merging into a trail, look uphill and yield to others.
5. Always use devices to help prevent runaway equipment.
6. Observe all posted signs and warnings. Keep off closed trails and out of closed areas.
7. Prior to using any lift, you must have the knowledge and ability to load, ride, and unload safely.

Endorsed by the National Ski Areas Association, Professional Ski Instructors of America, National Ski Patrol, American Association of Snowboard Instructors, American Ski Federations, United States Ski Industries Association, Cross-Country Ski Areas Association, United States Ski Association, Ski Coach's Association and other organizations.

AVALANCHE BAIT

Skiers also make great **avalanche** bait. Every year, avalanches kill skiers. Almost all of the deaths happen out-of-bounds—beyond the ski resort's marked area. Today, many big resorts offer **off-piste** or ungroomed trails, so you can experience natural skiing in-bounds.

Ski patrol teams regularly check these rugged off-piste slopes for avalanche conditions. Sometimes resorts set off avalanches with explosives to prevent unexpected snow slides later.

Off-piste skiers wear transceivers, or peeps, for added safety. If an avalanche buries a skier wearing a transceiver, the rescue teams can follow the beeps coming from under the snow. Skiers also carry shovels and use poles that double as probes to poke into deep snow. That's how they find the victims.

Never ski out-of-bounds. Always ski with a buddy. Your life depends on it.

Off-piste skiing lets advanced skiers experience nature's best ... and worst.

In-line skating uses many of the same muscles as downhill skiing does.

OFF-SEASON TRAINING

Even when the snow melts, skiers train for skiing. Find other sports to keep your body tuned for better skiing next winter. Look for cross-training sports that require balance. Some sports use the same muscles as skiing. Others use the same motions. Just stay active!

DAREDEVIL TRICKS

Skiing has always had its daredevils. The first person to strap his feet onto two long, skinny wooden planks and speed across the snow probably wasn't your average couch potato, right?

History's first extreme skiers found fame during Norway's civil war in 1206. Two Vikings wearing long, skinny skis rescued a baby prince from invaders and skied 55 kilometers (34.4 miles) to safety. They used no poles.

chapter
FOUR

THE OLD SCHOOL

Downhill skiing became a popular sport in the 1960s when technology improved the lifts, snow groomers, and snow-making machines. Young skiers with attitudes flocked to the ski resorts looking for thrills. They created the action-packed freestyle skiing.

Now called "Old School," freestyle skiing of the '60s and '70s focused on moguls, **aerial** tricks, and ballet skiing. Moguls—man-made bumps of snow as large as cars—challenged skiers ripping down the slopes.

These extreme skiers, called hotdoggers, soon added aerial tricks to their runs. Some hotdoggers only did tricks off big jumps. Freestyle skiing had few rules and a lot of danger.

SCORNED!

Early hotdoggers faced the same scorn that today's snowboarders, freeskiers, and skiboarders do. The International Ski Federation didn't officially accept freestyle skiing until 1979. The mogul competition finally joined the Olympics at the Albertville Games in 1992. Aerials followed in 1994.

The word "mogul" comes from combining MOuntains and GULlies. Moguls are also called "whoop-de-dos" or "whoops."

Mogul competitions still keep the extreme attitude flying high.

STILL WILD

Today's mogul competitions push skiers to really sharpen their skiing skills and their tricks. Hotdoggers seem to dance through the moguls as they make tight, fast turns. Judges look for speed, skill, **creativity** and gracefulness. Each skier takes two jumps on the way down. Style with big-air moves will turn the judges' heads.

Aerial competitions steal the show. Huge kickers, or jumps, pop skiers as high as 45 feet (13.7 m) into the air. Hotdoggers perform upright aerials, keeping their heads above their feet. Upright aerials include spins, twists and spreads. These skiers also try for **inverted** aerials, such as flips and somersaults. More than one guy has landed three backward somersaults and four twists off a single kicker!

TRAINING BUILDS SKILLS

When you watch a freestyle event, you might think it looks more like a carnival than a serious contest. Loud music blares from speakers. Hotdoggers dress in wild colors and patterns. They act more like entertainers than athletes sometimes. However, they train with strict programs to safely build their skills. Using trampolines and man-made ski hills paired with water landings, these skiers practice their tricks over and over again during the summer before they move onto the snow.

FREESTYLE TRICKS

Look for these tricks during freestyle mogul and aerial competitions.
- Back Scratcher: Both knees bend up so the ski tails touch on the skier's back.
- Daffy: The legs spread apart like a running stride.
- Kosak: A split in the air.
- Quad triple: Four somersaults and three twists in the air.
- Helicopter: A 360-degree turn in the air.
- Spread Eagle: The legs and arms spread out in the air.

Judges watch for amplitude, or height, of a jump.
They also look for creativity and style.

JONNY MOSELEY RULES BOTH SCHOOLS

A competitor since he was 12 years old, Jonny Moseley mastered the Old School freestyle skiing when he was young. He holds a long list of championships, especially in moguls. In 1998, Jonny stunned Olympic judges with a basic mute grab during his freestyle mogul run in Nagano, Japan. He took home the gold medal.

After Nagano, Jonny crossed over to New School's freeskiing. He quickly became one of the top North American jibbers. He hosts the Jonny Moseley Invitational Skiercross/Huck-for-bucks event and draws some of the biggest names in big-air skiing today.

Jonny plans to train for mogul competitions again. Watch for him in the Olympics and in ski movies. But, most importantly, watch how he blurs the lines between freestyle and freeskiing. You don't have to stick with Old School or New School.

Jonny Moseley, one of the world's best skiers, does a basic mute grab during a freestyle competition. He also wins freeskiing competitions.

FREE TO SKI

Jonny (Big Air, Air Time) Moseley has won competitions in freestyle moguls, slopestyle, and freeskiing Big Air. Freestyle? Freeskier? Whatever you call him, he just wants to be free to ski!

Born: 8/27/75
Height: 5'11" (180 cm)
Weight: 180 lbs. (81.6 kg)
Hometown: Tiburon, CA
Started skiing: Age 4
First Competition: 1987

NEW SCHOOL LESSONS

Skiing changes all the time. For awhile, skiing seemed like snowboarding's dull country cousin. "New Schoolers" hit the terrain parks and half-pipes full force in the 1990s and pushed skiing back into the spotlight.

TRICK TALK

Freeskiing and skiboarding focus on awesome tricks—some borrowed from snowboarding. Unlike snowboarders, skiers work two boards at the same time during a trick. If you take a jump, tuck your knees up for more air. Once you're in the tuck, your ski tips naturally cross. Uncross them before you land! Always scout your landing zone before you try a new jump. Blindly jumping off a cliff could kill you.

BASIC TRICKS

1. Grabs, or holding (not just touching) a ski or skiboard at the tip, tail, or center.
2. The fakie, or riding backwards, is more difficult than it looks. Skiboarders learn to ride fakie very early on—sometimes the first day!

Grabs like this one add style to your tricks. Notice that this freeskier uses no poles.

In a spin, your head leads the turn.

3. Spins, starting with the 180 (say: one-eighty), get bigger with practice. Use your math skills here. A full circle is 360 degrees. So a half spin is 180. A double spin equals what?

INTERMEDIATE TRICKS

1. Grinding means sliding sideways or forward on a rail in the snow, usually in the snowboard park. You jump onto the rail and let your momentum carry you across.
2. Combining any two basic tricks in the half-pipe shows you're no newbie.

ADVANCED TRICKS

Flips or other inverted maneuvers. If you're good enough to do them, you'll figure them out.

HAPPY HUCKING

Hucking, pulling air, usually includes tricks. Resorts make tabletop jumps with a curving take off for the launch and a clear landing area. Too much speed shoots the skier past the landing, where the most serious injuries happen.

Know your landing. It's not enough to spot it when you're up in the air. Check for cliffs, rocks and trees before you launch. Expert freeskiers also recommend that you always ski a jump the first time just for air—no tricks. Scoping the landing this way helps you to judge how much speed to take on.

WORKING THE HALF-PIPE

Freeskiers and skiboarders pop off jumps fairly easily. Tricks in the half-pipe take more work. Half-pipes, and the new Superpipes, become rock-hard by the season's end in some parts of the country. This solid ice resists edging. Ski patrollers haul a lot of broken ribs and sprained wrists out of the half-pipe then. Watch for changing conditions.

Most ski resorts ban inverted tricks, or upside-down moves. Dial in your basic tricks first; then move up to more difficult moves. When you think you're ready for a flip, find a good ski camp. Camp pros can show you how to nail the sickest tricks without mushing your melon.

COMPETITION FEVER

Once called Extreme Skiing, the New School has fired up skiers and audiences worldwide. ESPN Winter X Games and Alaska's World Extremes in the United States, European Extremes in France, plus countless other demonstrations, **exhibitions** and regional competitions draw athletes and fans to the slopes. The contests change as the sport grows. You may see some of these contests on TV or even at your local ski resort.

chapter
FIVE

BIG AIR CONTESTS

Defying gravity and common sense, Big Air skiers and skiboarders try to launch the biggest and most technical tricks and still land upright. They try for mid-air grabs, flips, and spinning tricks packed with style. Then they stomp their landings. Judges look for creativity, control, technical skill, and, of course, style.

Big Air competitions show off skiing skills and creativity.
Style makes the difference between good and great.

MORE WAYS TO WIN

SkierX Competitions

SkierX is like Slopestyle with a NASCAR® attitude. Unleashed from the gate at the same time, six skiers rip down a course and jostle for position. They hit jumps to gain ground—not to do tricks.

Slopestyle Contest

Skiers jam through a fast terrain park, hitting different shaped jumps and metal rails. Judges rank them based on air, style, tricks, and overall impression.

Speed and skill set SkierX racers apart from other freeskiers.

KRISTEN ULMER: ONE OF FREESKIING'S FAVORITE FEMALES

A skier since age 7, Kristen Ulmer caught the media's attention as a world-class mogul champion. She skied on the U.S. Ski Team until 1991. Then she moved on to full-time freeskiing, doing stunts and chasing down rugged backcountry terrain. Her specialty is ski mountaineering, a blend of rock climbing up steep mountains and death-defying skiing back down.

The first woman to ski Wyoming's craggy Grand Teton, Kristen keeps looking for fresh adventures all over the world. She also writes about her thrilling trips, skis for movies, and promotes her sponsors (Atomic skis, Scott goggles, Leki poles, and Red Bull energy drink).

Competitive skiers like Kristen face non-stop dangers. They have the skills to make smart choices about speed, cold, **obstacles,** and other risks. Follow their examples and use your brain when you ski. Your body will thank you for it.

Kristen Ulmer
Born: Sometime around 1966
Height: 5'8"(172.7 cm)
Weight: 145 lbs. (65.8 kg)
Hometown: Little Cottonwood Canyon, UT
Began skiing: Age 7

FURTHER READING

Your library and the Internet can help you learn more about snow skiing. Check these titles and sites for starters:

Ayers, Rebecca W., ed. *PSIA Alpine Manual*. Professional Ski Instructors of America Education Foundation, 1996.

Skiing Magazine
Freeskier magazine

WEBSITES TO VISIT

www.aaacwj.com

www.englishbay.com

www.bcfreestyle.com

EXPN.go.com

www.freeskionline.com

CBS.Sportsline.com

www.1080skiboarding.com

www.skiboarding.org

www.skiboardsonline.com

www.KristenUlmer.com

www.worldskiboardfederation.com

www.skiingmag.com

www.freeskier.com

GLOSSARY

aerial (AYR ee uhl) — a trick performed in the air

avalanche (AV uh lanch) — a large area of snow that breaks free and plows down the mountain like a mud slide

bevel (BEV ul) — an edge cut at an angle

creativity (kree ay TIV uh tee) — original thinking, new ideas

exhibitions (ek sa BISH unz) — events that show off the performers' talents, usually without awarding prizes

hypothermia (hy poh THUR mee ah) — cold, below-normal body temperature

inverted (in VURT id) — upside down; inverted tricks include flips and somersaults

lateral (LAT ur ul) — side-to-side movement or balance

moguls (MOH gulz) — bumps, some as big as cars, made from snow

newbie (NOO bee) — a person new at a sport, such as skiing

obstacles (AHB stuh kilz) — things blocking a path; in skiing, this includes jumps, moguls and trees

off-piste (AWF peest) — ungroomed trails

pressure (PRESH ur) — weight or force placed onto an object by pushing or pressing

quadriceps (KWAD reh seps) — muscles on the tops of your thighs

resistant (rih ZIS tant) — able to withstand or guard against something

responsibility (reh spon sah BILL ah tee) — a duty; knowing right from wrong

telemark (TEL ah mark) — a style of skiing often related to cross-country skiers who ski downhill

INDEX

ABOUT THE AUTHOR

Tracy Nelson Maurer specializes in nonfiction and business writing. Her most recently published children's books include the *A to Z* series, also from Rourke Publishing LLC. An avid skier since age 4, she lives with her husband Mike and two children in Superior, Wisconsin.